First American Edition 1986 by Kane/Miller Book Publishers
Brooklyn, New York & La Jolla, California

Originally published in England in 1986 by Andersen Press Ltd.
Copyright © Tony Ross 1986

All rights reserved. For information contact:
Kane/Miller Book Publishers
P.O. Box 529, Brooklyn, New York 11231

Library of Congress Cataloging-in-Publication Data

Ross, Tony.
I want my potty.

"A Cranky Nell book."
Summary: a little princess, tired of diapers,
learns to use the potty, although it's not always
easy.
[1. Toilet training—Fiction] I. Title.
PZ7.R71992Iac   1986   [E]   86-10568
ISBN 0-916291-08-1

Printed and bound in Italy by New Interlitho S.P.A. Milan
1 2 3 4 5 6 7 8 9 10

I Want My Potty

Tony Ross

A CRANKY NELL BOOK

 Kane/Miller Book Publishers

Brooklyn, New York & La Jolla, California

"Diapers are YUUECH!" said the little princess.
"There MUST be something better!"

"The potty's the place," said the queen.

At first the little princess thought the potty was
worse.

"THE POTTY'S THE PLACE!" said the queen.

So . . . the little princess had to learn.

Sometimes the little princess was a long way from the potty when she needed it most.

Sometimes the little princess played tricks on the potty . . .

. . . and sometimes the potty played tricks on the little princess.

Soon the potty was fun

and the little princess loved it.

Everybody said the little princess was clever and
would grow up to be a wonderful queen.

"The potty's the place!" said the little princess proudly.

One day the little princess was playing at the top of
the castle . . . when . . .

"I WANT MY POTTY!" she cried.

"She wants her potty," cried the maid.

"She wants her potty," cried the king.

"She wants her potty," cried the cook.

"She wants her potty," cried the gardener.

"She wants her potty," cried the general.

"I know where it is," cried the admiral.

So the potty was taken as quickly as possible

to the little princess . . . just

. . . a little too late.